THIS BOOK IS DEDICATED TO BETTYE SHELTON. FOR BY THE GRACE OF GOD SHE PUT ALL THE ELEMENTS TOGETHER FOR THIS STORY TO BECOME A BOOK. HER LOVE AND DEDICATION TO THIS STORY MAKES IT POSSIBLE FOR ALL TO ENJOY. FOR THIS I THANK YOU.

ALSO FOR MY DUCKS, PEANUT BUTTER AND QUACKER. "QUACK! QUACK!" (THAT'S DUCK TALK FOR THANK YOU.)

ALSO FOR MY ARTIST, SHAN WILLIAMS, WHOM GOD SENT TO ME. FOR SHE BROUGHT THE STORY ALIVE!

THANK YOU EVERYONE!

THERE ONCE WAS A DUCK
NAMED QUACKER
WHO WOULD WAG HIS TAIL LIKE A DOG.

IT SEEMED SO STRANGE,
IN THE SUN...

...OR THE RAIN
THAT A DUCK
WOULD WAG HIS TAIL AT ALL!

COULD IT BE
THAT QUACKER WAS ALL MIXED UP,
AND THOUGHT HE WAS A PUP
INSTEAD OF A DUCK?

I DON'T THINK SO,
SAID A BOY NAMED JOE,
FOR I KNEW HIS BROTHERS AND SISTERS.

THEY ALL HAD FEATHERS
AND THEY ALL
COULD SWIM,...

THEY ALL COULD FLY,
AND THEY LOOKED
LIKE HIM.

SO QUACKER MUST HAVE LEARNED
TO WAG HIS TAIL,
FROM LUCKY AND ZEUS, THE DOGS.

WHILE PLAYING IN THE WOODS,
AND DOWN BY THE POND,
AND OVER THE STUMPS AND LOGS.

I THINK I'LL ASK, SAID THE BIRD TO THE BEE, AS THEY STARED AT QUACKER SITTING UNDER THE TREE.

QUACKER, ARE YOU REALLY A DUCK?
IF SO, WHY DO YOU WAG YOUR TAIL
LIKE A PUP?

So Quacker just stared them
in the eyes,
And said, Mr. Bird, Mr. Bee,
Sitting in that Sycamore tree
Why do you want to know about me?

IF I FLAP MY WINGS OR WAG MY TAIL
OR LOOK FOR A BUG INSIDE A SHELL,
IT'S JUST ME, IT'S JUST MY WAY
I WAG MY TAIL MOST EVERYDAY!

AND WHEN I TALK,
I HONK AND QUACK,
LOOK STRAIGHT AHEAD, NEVER BACK!

THERE ARE NO RULES
FOR A WAY TO BE.
JUST BE YOURSELF, SIT IN YOUR TREE.

BEE, YOU BUZZ; AND BIRD, YOU CHIRP,
I WAG MY TAIL,
AND LITTLE KIDS BURP!

IT'S JUST A LITTLE THING I DO,
BUT I WILL STOP
IF IT BOTHERS YOU.

NO, PLEASE DON'T STOP!
YOU WAG YOUR TAIL!
WE UNDERSTAND,
AND THINK IT'S SWELL.

BUT YOU CANNOT KNOW
IF YOU DO NOT ASK
AND SO WE DID
AND NOW IT'S PASSED.

SO GOODBYE SAID BIRD,
GOODBYE, SAID BEE;
WE'LL TELL THE REST...

...WHO LOOK AND SEE
AND SAY IT'S FINE
TO BE YOURSELF!

IN THE NEXT STORY,
QUACKER MEETS MRS. MOO!